I0814918

THIS BOOK IS GIFTED TO

YOU HUNG THE MOON

A LOVE LETTER BETWEEN MOTHER AND CHILD

Jessica Urlichs and Sarah Reinhardt

RIGHT NOW IT'S JUST US,
IT'S JUST YOU AND I,
AND THE BEAUTIFUL MOON
UP ABOVE IN THE SKY.

AND WHEN YOU HOLD ME
AND SWAY LIKE YOU DO,
I KNOW IT WAS YOU
WHO HUNG THE MOON.

IN YOUR EMBRACE,
AS WE SPEND TIME TOGETHER,
I KNOW THIS IS TRUE:
I WILL LOVE YOU FOREVER.

YOU'RE MY WHOLE WORLD.
YOU'RE PERFECT TO ME.
YOU SHINE LIKE THE STARS.
YOU'RE ALL THAT I SEE.

WHATEVER WE DO,
WHATEVER WE'RE SEEING,
AS LONG AS WE'RE TOGETHER,
WITH YOU I LOVE BEING.

C
A
B

AND NOW I CAN MOVE
A BIT FURTHER EACH DAY.
BUT WHEREVER I GO,
YOU'RE NOT TOO FAR AWAY.

AS THE YEARS PASS,
I DO MORE THINGS ALONE.
IN YOUR ARMS I WILL SOFTEN,
YOU STILL FEEL LIKE HOME.

THE DAYS ARE NOW SHORTER,
MY HUGS NOT AS LONG.
THE WORLD SEEMS SO BIG
AS WE JOURNEY ALONG.

FOR NOW I'LL STILL SEARCH
FOR YOUR FACE IN A CROWD.
THROUGH THE WINS AND THE LOSSES
I KNOW YOU'RE STILL PROUD.

BECAUSE A MOTHER'S LOVE
SHINES BRIGHT IN THE DARK,
THE KIND THAT I FEEL
EVEN WHEN WE'RE APART.

AND WHEN I FEEL ILL,
NO MATTER WHAT, THERE IS YOU.
YOU STILL GIVE ME COMFORT.
YOU ALWAYS KNOW WHAT TO DO.

MOBY DICK

WHEN MY WORLD FEELS TOO HEAVY,
YOU HELP CALM MY FEAR.
YOU TEACH ME SO MUCH
BY SIMPLY BEING HERE.

THE YEARS WILL PASS BY
AND WE MAY DISAGREE.
WE MIGHT EVEN DRIFT APART
AS I WORK OUT WHAT'S 'ME'.

BUT YOU'RE STILL MY CONSTANT,
EVEN ON THE WORST DAYS.
I'LL ALWAYS NEED YOU, MUM,
JUST IN DIFFERENT WAYS.

SOMETIMES YOU'LL WORRY
AND I UNDERSTAND WHY,
BUT DON'T BE AFRAID:
BECAUSE OF YOU, I CAN FLY.

I WILL BE BACK.
NOT AS YOUNG, NOT YET OLD.
STILL YOUR BABY, YOU'LL SAY,
BUT MUCH HEAVIER TO HOLD.

THE SEASONS WILL CHANGE,
AND AS EACH LEAF FALLS,
IT'S OUR MEMORIES I WILL TAKE
FOR MY VERY OWN WALLS.

I'LL FIND MY SOMEONE,
A NEW HAND TO HOLD.
IN A CHAPTER OF MY OWN,
A NEW STORY WILL UNFOLD.

WHILE I'LL MISS YOU A BIT,
I AM ON MY WAY.
YESTERDAY'S GOODBYES
ARE THE HELLOS OF TODAY.

WHEN I SEE YOU AGAIN,
LET'S MAKE THE TIME LAST.
LET'S LAUGH OVER MEMORIES.
LET'S CELEBRATE OUR PAST.

FOR SOON I'LL DISCOVER
THE WORK BEHIND THE SCENES.
ALL YOU'VE DONE FOR ME,
I'LL UNDERSTAND WHAT IT MEANS.

DID I TELL YOU ENOUGH?
YOU ARE SUCH A GOOD MUM.
I HOPE YOU ARE PROUD
OF ALL I'VE BECOME.

MY LOVE IS AS FAR
AS THE SUN'S BRIGHTEST RAYS,
AS BIG AS THE UNIVERSE
AND AS LONG AS ALWAYS.

SUCH A BLUR ARE THESE DAYS,
BUT THIS MUCH IS TRUE:
JUST AS THEY NEED ME,
I STILL NEED YOU.

BECAUSE THIS BEAUTIFUL LIFE,
THIS LOVE LIKE NO OTHER,
IT BEGAN WITH YOU.
IT BEGAN WITH A MOTHER.

NOW IT'S OUR TURN, SWEET BABY,
IT'S JUST ME AND YOU
AND THE NIGHT SKY ABOVE,
WHERE YOU HUNG THE MOON.

FOR ALL THE MOTHERS,
ESPECIALLY MINE.
— J.U.

FOR MY MUM AND MY GRANNIES,
YOU MEAN THE WORLD TO ME.
— S.R.

A Little Moa Book
Published in New Zealand in 2023
by Hachette Aotearoa New Zealand
(an imprint of Hachette New Zealand Limited)
Level 2, 23 O'Connell Street, Auckland, New Zealand
www.hachette.co.nz

A catalogue record for this book is available
from the National Library of New Zealand.

978-1-86971-487-1 (hardback)

Cover and internal design by Sarah Reinhardt
Printed in China by Toppan Leefung Printing Limited